The Oracle

Being the First Part of

Elder Tree

By

R. A. Holihan

Illustrated by Dan Holihan

Published in Yellow Springs, Ohio, by Ready Writer Books.

Cover artwork and illustrations done by Dan Holihan.

Printed in the United States of America

ISBN-13: 978-0615929699
ISBN-10: 0615929699

Table of Contents

Introduction

Imagine you happened upon writings that revealed the Wisdom of ancient cosmological understanding from cultures spanning continents and millenniums. Imagine that these writings conveyed in esoteric and poetic form the mysterious understanding of sacred texts and held beliefs of antiquarian philosophers of stars and calendars. Now suppose that, like the layers of a city that has been covered for millenniums, these writings were the lost and forgotten foundation of Wisdom literature that revealed the commonalities between cosmological understandings of the nature of God. If these traditions were unearthed, they would be the discovery of a mysterious and once-held system of thought. The Wisdom of this lost knowledge of the ancients would be essential to cultivating a clear and precise paradigm of the hidden treasure of ancient cosmologies.

Elder Tree is a mystical concept and reference to the disciples and initiates who knew the secrets of the cosmos and the nature of God. As an epistle, Elder Tree is an ancient, esoteric expression of inspirational, spiritual and philosophical understanding about God and the world. The tale spans the knowledge of various cultures familiar with the heavenly inspiration of The Oracle, emulating the cosmolgical concepts of antiquity.

Book one, The Oracle, is both sage wisdom and the

artistry found in sacred lore.

This work is not intended to defend a particular model of cosmology or establish proof, scientific theory or philosophical debate. This was never the intent of the writers of the time. Cosmology was a belief system based on an understanding of being and knowing as it related to the nature of God and the origin of the universe. Cosmology encompassed both the natural world and the unseen world, establishing a geogalactic view of the cosmos. The philosophy of antiquarian traditions incorporated into science a study of infinite horizons. As one who sits in the shade of the Elder Tree, my hope is for you to navigate your way through these infinite horizons to find yourself in the presence of the King of the Universe.

-Rebecca

ACKNOWLEDGEMENTS

Nothing we do in life comes solely on our own. I realized early on that it would take a team to accomplish my goals for Elder Tree. I want to thank my lead editor, Sarah Smith for the hard work and dedication of keeping me in voice and celebrating with me my strengths along the way. Her generous advice and coaching helped make sense of this very esoteric project. I want to thank my second editor, Annie Hoke, for her diligence and support in polishing the rough edges of this work. Annie was able to burnish the pages till they glistened. I would like to thank A.J. Hoke for transcribing my meditative journal notes of more than ten years that I was able to weave throughout the fabric of The Oracle.

To my two sons, Michael and Taylor Smith, who are inspirations as writers in their own rite. Thank you bunches! Michael has been a tremendous encouragement in the original music used in Elder Tree. A fantastic musician himself, I have deeply appreciated his assistance in recording and coaching along the way. Taylor assisted in the editing and formatting of this project and has encouraged me immensely whenever I was struggling with my writing. His eye for detail and the countless hours invested in this project was invaluable to the finish of this work. Taylor's own poetry has been an example of sensitivity and brilliance that I desire to emulate.

To all my family and friends who have patiently and kindly supported me with faithful hearts to the finish of this most rewarding work, I am truly grateful. All my lovin'!

To my husband, Dan, who held up my arms through the years of research and study. Dan created all the amazing art illustrations. Thanks for all the times you listened endlessly to my research, thoughts, writing and a crazy idea to go back to school to formalize all that I have had passion for in music, poetry and art. Crazy ideas? Don't you just love those!

Finally, all my love and adoration to the Father of Lights of whom I have been an initiate, disciple, and student. I have tried faithfully to scribe the things He has shared with me in secret about cosmology. To Him be the glory!

I watched you sleeping under Elder Trees—Ancient
Pines bowing down overhead
Sleep came easy on summer dreams
Resting on a pine-needle bed
Secluded and sacred this place that we found
Like the breath-taking awe of cathedrals
Twirling and spinning we fell to the ground
As the trees hovered over like angels
I watched you sleeping under Elder Trees—Ancient
Pines bowing down overhead
I pray I share wisdom far older than trees
That dance like dreams in your head

All the songs, prayers, and poetry of Elder Tree
were written by the author. All other quotations are
italicized and referenced in the endnotes.

Dedicated to my children's children

On Wisdom

A wise man will hear and increase learning
And a man of understanding will attain wise counsel,
To understand a proverb and an enigma
The words of the wise and their riddles

My son, if you accept my words and treasure this revelation in your heart, you will gain Wisdom more valuable than gold. This oracle is built on the mysteries of the ancients, cultivated in secret and is given to you from the age-old foundations of the genesis. If you gain understanding and store up this knowledge, you will understand truth from the storehouses of heaven.

In secret, the Father of Lights formed that which was invisible and made it corporeal. By His wisdom, He reveals that time has an essential component as well as an eternal postulate determined and complete by the One who stands outside of the void. *For by Him all things consist and are held together.* Before there was air, He breathed. Before there was fire, light essence pierced the dark. Water had no substance before His vibration and man had no image before He spoke. From the utterance of His mouth the conception of all things was made manifest, for the Creator is the cornerstone upon which the foundations of the worlds were built. With great humility, I have searched for truth from the One who is the Alpha and Omega, the Eternal. The Maker of the Universe binds the cluster of the Pleiades and loosens the Belt of Orion. He alone has set the ordinances of the heavens and established His sovereignty over all things. The King of the Universe envelops all that exists and all that exists emanates from His light. Only He who created signs and seasons can be revered for such dominion.

Keep sound Wisdom, my son and you will increase in learning and understanding. Those who abide in her are like the Elder Tree that is *planted by streams of water, that brings forth its fruit in season and whose leaf does not wither.* Wisdom will lead your feet on a straight path into all truth. She will be health to your body and life to your soul. *The Lord by Wisdom founded the earth; by understanding He established the heavens.* All these truths of the Father of Lights, my son, were spoken by the sisters of Alexandria and the Sybil poets who prophesied in the days of Noah:

> *First now God urges on me to relate*
> *Truly how into being came the world*
> *And thou, shrewd mortal, prudently make known,*
> *Lest ever thou should'st my commands neglect,*

4

The King most high, who brought into existence
The whole world saying, "Let there be", and there
was.
For he the earth established, placing it
Round about Tartartus, and he himself
Gave the sweet light; he raised the heavens on high,
Spread out the gleaming sea and covered the sky.

You must learn, my son, that nothing breeds nothing. The design, beauty and order of the cosmos demand a designer. If you listen with a desire to gain Wisdom, you will understand that I am giving you the pillars of the ancients and the foundational principles that mark the genesis of all things. Within the culture of the ancients, hidden mysteries were revealed as far as the east is from the west. These were archetypes of what the men of old knew of the origins of all things. From the time of the original language these oral traditions were handed down. It was a time of the unity of thought about the stars, the powers in the heavens and the world of mankind. Only when man sought his own way and pursued the making of towers to the heavens did The King of the Universe scatter their thoughts and speech to the four corners of the earth. It was a time of chaos, as man sought power and dominion over the stars of the skies.

Since that time, known to all of antiquity, the kings and tribes of the earth began to establish myth and legend out of vain imaginations. All manner of chronology of the origins sprung like water from below the earth. Man began to carve on tablets of stone, stories in symbol and number, which attempted to mirror the truth of the genesis. These reflections made in man's image were birthed in the murky waters of his soul, seeking power to be like his Maker. Though many tried to remember the beginning of all things, they held to fading dreams and visions of the original design. Like an ocean mist, the secrets of oath and sequential patterns spoken from God's breath had all but dissipated from his memory. Now all who believed in the deceptive and empty philosophies of the nature of the cosmos would see as one looking through a glass dimly.

The secret teachings of sages and the orators of mysticism would prophesy, setting the standard for mathematical postulates and universal harmony, corrupting the thoughts of man and mingling truth with fiction. The temple priests tried to piece together the fragments that made up the fabric of antediluvian patterns and cycles, of wheels within wheels and of a sacred language lost. Men of vain philosophies would create tales that became the bread to feed hungry students and create a thirst for the deep wells of thought found in the oral traditions of times past. Like a mirage in a desert, their thirst could not be quenched by imagination, nor their hunger be fed by the understanding of man's making.

Man began to erode the truth of what the God of the universe had designed in His infinite Wisdom. The sorcerers of Persia and the Chaldean wizards would conjure philosophies of the stars to suit the bellies of kings. The darkened form of Wisdom would be passed from generation to generation, from poet to sophist in an age when they would forever be searching but never finding, listening but never hearing. Until man bows a knee to the will and worship of his Maker, he will navigate past the vast depths of truth and find himself in the abyss of dark waters, for out of the mysteries of the heavenly realms descends the still, small voice of the Ancient of Days with secrets revealed to the trusted ones of old. These fathers of Wisdom scribed of the storehouses of heaven, the patterns of wind and snow and the oracles that spoke of fallen angels who were thrown out of the heavenly kingdom. In those days, the scribes of The Most High taught of a heavenly alliance, which set out to bring corruption to earth and man, with deception and the promise of power greater than the Maker of the Universe. Many were the children of men who blindly embraced the magic of the fallen angels over miracle, and the fruit of good and evil over life, which flowed from streams of living water. They did not lift their eyes to the heavens from where all manner of help comes, but they conceived their own glory attempted to corrupt the great design, leaving man in a veil of deception.

Many were the great mysteries that were shared in secret by the seers and prophets of the King of the Universe. Those who held to the Wisdom of His glory and majesty handed down the knowledge to their children and their children's children. They shared these truths in story and song as in the Hymn of Ascension:

Sing with harp and bowl my son
Sing a new song of ascension
With prayerful heart we light the incense
With joyful lyre make proclamation
Of the One who gave us reason
Who from His speech all things were made
He is light without a shadow
Who was and is and is to come
Immerse yourself in all His splendor
Adorn His truth around your neck
Find the path of His great Wisdom
Praise the Craftsman for His art.

The path of Wisdom flowing from humble hearts gives rise to understanding the harmony and unity found in the cosmic framework. The splendor of the cosmos is arrayed with beauty and majesty that was established and formed in singularity from the fingerprint of the Creator. The dynamic principle of these histories reveals to us a genesis, a starting point of the worlds of God's making and speaks to us of His nature. He who sits above the circle of the earth determined the boundaries of the universe and set the course of the spheres. He removes the veil that separates heaven and earth. Through Him the quest for truth is made known. He illuminates the celestial mysteries of time and nature. The hand of the Maker establishes singularity. Without His power, unity is without understanding. Matter and energy would cease to exist and all the landscape of magnitude and force that connect the worlds and are held in balance would be nothing. He is the Almighty. He alone is the source of life. Only by His presence, infused with His divine light, can the constructs of time find significance in relationship to all the forces of the universe, those inside the realm of creation and those in the heavenly realms that permeate it. Man's significance and purpose to the Creator is found in relationship to Him, *for by Him and to Him and through Him are all things.* As The King of the Universe spoke in times past, "I am that I am," God cannot be punctuated.

This mystery of God and His creation is illuminated through Wisdom, yet few find the path to her door. Wisdom opens the eyes of our heart to all the enigmas that rise above our understanding. These riddles of the cosmos unfold as one ascends in spirit into heavenly realms. Though she speaks to us of things beyond our capacity, it must be known that the Wisdom of the ages is timeless and one with the Ruler of the heavens. She is the very nature of God Himself and cannot be revealed by lessons in reason disputed by the quadrivium circles of sophists. Those who diminish the cosmos to precepts of reason see only glimpses of truth through the windows of the heavens. Here I must caution you, my son, and all who read this oracle. Wisdom makes herself known to man and only in vanity does man try to subdue her as if she could be held captive in man's thoughts and displayed in the marketplace as a prize of wit in the chatter of boastful dialogue. These poets of astronomy and mathematics, who entertain philosophies of the universe, build their understanding on oracles of unknown gods, for the entertainment of such rhetoric is infinitesimal to the mystery of God's Wisdom. The divine nature is not formed from the hand of a sculptor or discovered in the temples at Delphi. Mankind is not the offspring of myth, nor do such imaginations evolve from the finite thoughts of man who make foolish claims about their Maker. Those of vast knowledge try to define Him as if He could be fathomed in their minds and spoken of as if He could be formed in their image. Such concepts are void of Wisdom; such claims are without experience. The nature of the universe is revealed to man from heaven to earth, from God's holy pavilion. He is the great potter who formed the worlds and sought to be mindful of us. The King of the Universe allows those who seek His face to be enlightened so that we might gain knowledge and awe of Him. Understand this, and you will be on Wisdom's path like the dreamer who carved these words in stone near a sacred portal:

> Descending from the heavens
> As upon a ladder
> To fill the man formed from the earth
> With breath and illumination
> To set him with an inner hunger
> To seek knowledge and discover
> Drawing him like stone to magnet
> Unto a heavenly ascension
> With anticipation to uncover
> The gold of Wisdom for the taking.

As you embark on this journey, my son, you will find that Wisdom leads you to the realms that transcend your reason, for the soul of man must become bound to the Wisdom of the Ruler of Heaven in order to become one in thought and deed. It is God's intention for man to ascend to heavenly realms and descend again, as on a ladder, to the world below to bear witness of the Light of the World. Our destiny is bound to Him and our devotion is surely to emulate His light and life to all men. As we pierce the heavens and find ourselves in these higher realms of spiritual enlightenment, we can arouse His nature as we draw close to Him. The King's intention is for us to carry His light back into a dark world where man can once again find

His way to the truth about the cosmos and the majesty of the One, for God loves the cosmos and all He created, stating it was good, holding back His judgment on us and shielding us from His immense power in order for us to find Him and serve Him all the days of our lives.

Our service to God is not merely good conduct as established in the schools of wise teachers or in the secret language of their initiates, for religion alone is but stale bread that will not last and shallow water that will not quench. Man must transcend the material world embracing awe of the Maker, for God is spirit and His substance is far above the corporeal realm of things seen. His thoughts are higher than ours and the fulfillment of our path lies in the journey that leads us back to Him who made the cosmos. His desire is *to reconcile man to himself making the two one.* Only when man comes to a place of such acknowledgment in word and deed will he begin to grasp the height of understanding and grasp the depth of his destiny, which was ordained before the foundations of the world. It is only by ascending in our spirit far beyond the horizons of this material world into the realm where all kingdom reality is made known that we can become the instrument of the Creator so that we can make a dwelling place for His presence in the world below. These mystics of old knew that the cosmic order was established to reveal the Ancient of Days and that the Children of

Men were designed to emulate His order in the world below, guiding his path into all truth of His love and goodness. Like fruit-bearing trees, we are called to scatter the seed of His goodness in all the earth. Let the song of the Elder Tree be our prayer:

> Hear the cry of the Lord's heart
> And worship at His feet
> Lift the yoke of oppression
> Serve the hurting ones in need
> Be a light in the darkness
> And a spring whose waters never fail
> And I know He will be there to guide you
> And I know He will strengthen your frame
> If you care for the poor and the dying
> Even the trees will whisper your name
> Even the trees will whisper your name—
> Selah.

We are but creatures of simplistic dimensions. The Lord is beyond the dimensions of the vast expanse of time. His divine essence cannot be determined nor can His ways be fully grasped; yet He has made a way for us to gain knowledge of the oracle of Wisdom to find understanding of the mysteries of His nature. Wisdom is food for your soul, my son, the place of hidden treasures.

> *I pray that you will be rooted and grounded in love,*
> *so that you, with all God's people, will be given*

strength to grasp the breadth, length, height and depth of God's love, yes, to know it, even though it is beyond all knowing, so that you will be filled with all the fullness of Him.

I urge you to be diligent in your search. Just as I have taken back the plunder of the riches of secret places, I exhort you to uncover the mysteries of the cosmos that you may know God in all His ways. This oracle is my gift to you. I set my face like flint with a passion to raise the age-old foundations. I have purposed in my heart a good theme to recite, so that in all that I do, *I make my tongue the pen of a ready writer to usher in the King of the Universe.*

On Light

He drew a circular horizon
on the face of the waters
at the boundary of light
and darkness

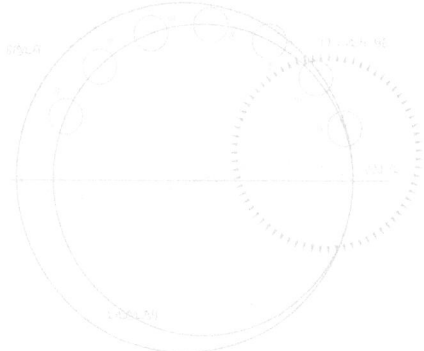

Consider this oracle and bind its truth around your neck, my son, concerning the light of the cosmos. Light essence, the light of the Creator, is invisible, immutable and unbegotten. Life did not spring from a vacuum nor was matter generated out of nothingness as if from a wisp of aether. Everything, visible and invisible, must be understood through the knowledge of light.

In the beginning, the Creator, who is light, established the realms of the universes by His light. He alone set the worlds in motion by His vibration, by His breath emanating the life essence of His brilliance. This is the light of life. All the luminaries are created forms of light, a mere reflection of the light of His being. Only from the Father's light is there life. Search for understanding, my son, and you will untangle the mysteries of light's essence that envelops all things corporeal.

From this teaching you must gain the

understanding, that what is seen mirrors the image of that which is unseen. Consider here the essence of light, which the Most High God created in the world of matter. The light essence, which is the Light of Life, is the very being of God Himself, generating substance and establishing matter, so that which is visible was fashioned out of that which is invisible. The first light of creation danced upon waves connecting particles and establishing time. Of all the elements, the primordial light does not evaporate or dissipate like water; it permeates all things. In an array of light's reflection we perceive the illumination of hidden substances, discover heat, and make sense of magnitudes and vibrations. Descending below the full spectrum of light's virtue, where the lower spheres of the heavens are determined by our senses, we gain Wisdom and knowledge of the finite world in which motion, velocity and time are measured. Within this realm, created light has limit and design set by the boundaries and borders inside the great circle of the earth, but the Light of the Father is far above man's reason to grasp. Yet, *in His light we see light.* Knowing this, keep your eyes lifted up.

One must ascend into the higher spheres of heaven, into the realms of higher dimensions to discover revelation of His light. In this domain, our thirsty spirits can drink from the depths of His living water and begin to grasp the mysteries unveiled by the King of the Universe. Only here can we perceive the inseparable energy of His nature and the power of His light, which is the source of life. Though at times hidden, shielding us from His immensity, the Father's light never decreases, for it is without measure, permeating all that exists. Like the sun whose rays stretch across the zenith of the morning and warm the earth, His light illuminates our path, for *He is the way, the truth and the life.* We are but a reflection of the one entity of all things.

Do not be ignorant, my son, when speaking of the genesis of created light, for out of the alchemy of thought, the Maker created the expanse. As His Spirit moved over the dark, there was a form of light predating the luminaries and the time clocks of the heavens. Buried in the depths of the oceans are the remnants of the genesis. Primordial light began in the subterranean gardens of the deep. The crystalline content of the waters established the first light known as luminescence. These streams were understood by the Children of Men as liquid light and mirrored in the heavens above. We know that the effervescence of God's Spirit descended over the waters, and from sequential constructs light was birthed. As recited by the children of the antediluvian world:

> Primordial Light—the early light—more ancient than the dawn of time—The luciferin light, the genetic code of creation descends The pillar of light that permeates the veil and

dissipates the dark
Poured into the deep and enveloped the
waters below
Bioluminescence baptizes the void as life
springs forth from living waters
From the alchemy of heaven illumination is
birthed
The first light ascends before the
governors—
Before the photosynthesis—the rulers of
signs and seasons
Within the great circle—deep calls to deep—
the beginning—the great awakening.

All these amazing wonders—light, substance,
dominions, powers and principalities, either visible
or invisible—were created by Him to reveal His
supremacy. Fire, water, air and earth are all created
elements of the cosmos, but the light essence of the
Ancient of Days is eternal. The essence of life is the
effervescence of His Spirit. It is the light of God's
nature that is the essential attribute to life. He is
the light that breathes life into all things. His
radiance gives design to the universe. All other
forms of light are mere reflections of His divine
omnipotence. The light of the I Am has no
beginning or end. There is no ability to measure or
qualify His divine essence, which is outside of time.
You cannot trace these substances back to His
being, for The Light of the World was not created.

Long after the earth had taken form, we understand that the luminaries of the heavens were created to mark the signs and seasons, but the remnants of God's primordial light at the dawn of creation, had its beginnings in the deep fathoms of the waters below. Not until the day when the veil that divided the earth from the heavens was seared did the poets of heaven sing the song of illumination about our unity the Maker of the Universe:

> Beyond the cosmic fabric of the veil
> Far above the circle that stretches over the new horizon
> Where jasper walls adorn the highest heaven
> And liquid light glistens over crystal waters
> The Veil
> In ceremony is removed
> Like a groom who lifts the gentle linen
> Covering the bride's sweet face
> It is the first kiss of oath
> The harmony of the spheres
> Many waters sing in testimony
> As virgin color permeates the world below
> And we with unveiled face
> Join in the dance
> The glory revealed
> The marriage of the One.

This limitless light of His glory is without

border or boundary, emanating His colors and patterns, pulsating through the universe and heard in the song of His stars. The Father of Lights penetrates to the core of all matter that make up His web of life. He births from His radiance all things new generated from His being alone. The harmony of the universe is in His hands on a grand scale of interlocking ideas and revealed order of His thoughts, for the sum of all that is the cosmos is contained in God. He established the hierarchical order of the spheres to demonstrate His splendor, for the mind of the Ancient of Days transcends the thoughts of His created beings. He is forever making petition for us to be drawn upward toward His divine intention for us, to understand His ways and to know Him, *for all who seek Him will find him if they seek Him with their whole heart.*

From those days till now, man has been caught in a web of illusion, theorizing about truth and dancing on shadows of the constructs of the Living God. From the craftiness that flowed from the mouth of the dark one, man was persuaded that the cosmos was birthed out of the created forces of nature, forsaking the truth that the power ruling the world is the light of the King of the Universe. Seek this out for yourself. God is the very essence of all things.

Observe the night sky, my son, and see that in all the heavens, the spheres, the stars, the galaxies, all things in heaven and on earth proclaim the one true light of life. For just as above where the unseen nature of the King of Glory dwells, so beneath the veil is the begotten, visible world of His creation. The entire universe sings of the Father of Lights and all His luminaries tell His story. For it is through this attribute of the King's light, which is the essence of life, that the world made its expansion. Through the very breath of His being the oracle of creation was formed. From this one eternal light we have the singularity of all things. Withdraw His light and there would be no expansion, no forces in the universe, there would be no creation, no worlds or purpose. The knowledge of light was known to all who understood the Wisdom of the ancients and sat in the counsel of the Elder Tree sages, whether kings or those in priestly garments.

So go forth, my son, and let your light shine before men. Find rest for your soul like one who finds rest in the shade of the Elder Tree. Seek and keep seeking, knock and keep knocking till you understand the width and depth and height of the knowledge and revelation of the oracle of light.

On Creation

Indeed these are the mere edges of His ways
and how small a whisper we hear of Him
But the thunder of His power
who can understand?

Share the understanding I have given you, my son, with all who desire to know truth. For the realm beyond the blue veil of the heavens, above the spheres of reasoning, is where you will come to know about the nature of creation. Glean from the fields of God's dominion and you will discover what is more valuable than gold, more precious than silver. Seek truth in these realms, and you will find the gate that reveals the origin of life and the keys to unlock the secrets of the universe. Through this entrance lie the answers to the genesis and the oneness of all things, for the Maker of the Universe is truth and life. If you find your way to His door, the truth will set you free.

To understand the secret truth that is found in this oracle requires Wisdom from the highest heavens. From this vantage point one can observe creation and its order, the patterns of things past and the expansion of the days to come. From the higher spheres one can sense the magnitude of the great design, the creation of time and the birth of man in the image of His Maker. Only from great heights does one come to understand the order of the cosmos, for it is heard in the music and the harmony of the governors, those stars and planets that sing of the beauty and majesty of the God of the Cosmic Order. This opera of the heavens illuminates understanding and creates alignment of the worlds above and below where light and sound establish the undertone and connectedness of all things. The harmonic circle that permeates the world is the background echo of God's primordial creation song. All that can be understood, all that is revealed to man has its origins in the word of the Almighty. His poetic sonnet formed the heavens, molded the earth and framed man from the dust of the earth. It is heard in the heavens and seen in His creation. The fragrance of His beauty fills the oceans, refreshes every sunset, and with each rising of the dawn, His goodness and mercy is ordered like a cosmic dance in the great continuum of the universe. Creation sings His praises: each tree of His garden, the lilies of the fields, from the birds of the air to every living creature, return in adoration the song that does not return void, making its way back to the great Creator who established everything in nature.

In the beginning, there was a garden where creation reflected God's image. In that garden were two trees: one of life and one of the knowledge of good and evil, that throughout the ages, peasant and king would draw near to those who told tales of the trees and the beginning of days. Storytellers and bards recited creation songs and oracles about the one true Maker of Heaven and Earth saying, *"To Him be the Kingdom, the power and the glory forever and ever!"* These ballads were spoken by the poets of old who boldly shared such words of reverence about heroes of great battles and men of renowned strength immortal as if any could compare to the Creator of all things. For the songs and stories of adoration were but a shadow of the beginning of days, a mere reflection of the love song about the King of the Universe and His creation.

> *Thou who, amid the trees of Eden, art a flowering myrtle tree,*
> *And amid the stars of heaven, art the bright Orion,*
> *God hath sent to thee a cluster of pure myrrh*
> *Of His own work, not the perfumer's skill.*
> *The dove from whom that day nested*
> *In the myrtle tree,*
> *The myrtle stole her fragrance and gave forth perfume—*
> *Ask not, while with her, for the sun to rise;*
> *She asketh not, with thee, for*
> *the rising of the moon.*

Since the time of the first garden, generations of

peoples began to expand across the earth, and from one to another, from father to son, the mysteries of the cosmos were revealed. They shared the stories of the stars and the revelation of man and beast, for the Children of Men knew of the dark one's plan to deceive and conjure spells, to corrupt the seed of man and to establish a conquest for the dominion of the heavens. This was a time of great sadness. Those who sought their own way, seeking to be like God Himself, fell into an abyss of lies. The people of the earth did not realize that nothing exists without His breath and nothing lives without His power, for He was known to all the begotten of His creation as the source and shield of life.

The music of the soul, like the vibration of the heavenly lights, reveals His order, beauty and unity with His creation. Though He is above all that He created, in His divine mercy He poured out His Spirit on all flesh so that man would be mindful of Him and worship the Creator of the world. It is only in this harmony that the world finds balance and enters into the cosmic dance that connects life and all of nature together. As we draw close to Him, the harmony of the spheres and the governors of the skies join together to declare His majesty as the life-giving force of nature. In gaining such Wisdom, one begins to discover movement and motion: the strength of the forces in heavenly realms, the meaning of number and symbol, color and patterns, of wheels within wheels, of the celestial framework of the universe. It is only when your eyes gaze beyond the realm of reason into the cosmic fabric of the unseen that your thoughts are illuminated. For as you move away from the earth in your spirit, there is a shift toward the full spectrum of His light, expanding your vision toward multi-colored horizons. This is where things are made complete in Him, both in the visible and invisible substance spoken by the fathers of Wisdom who remind us of our nature and life found only in Him.

> He hid me in His quiver and shot me as an
> arrow
> Out of the womb and into the begotten
> world of His creation
> Being mindful of me even before I was
> His breath—my substance
> He the eternal—and I the everlasting.

So from the time of Eden to this very day, man has understood the prophecy of these heavenly orbs, which conveyed the offspring of the promised seed of the Eternal One, He who was and is and is to come, who is the Son of Man and Son of God. Throughout the ages, men of great wealth and power, have sought to set up such a ruler. But those who were wise knew the Son was reavealed in the realm of the stars and prophesied by the King of the Universe: *And I will put enmity between you and the woman and between your seed and her seed; He shall bruise your head and you shall bruise His heel.* But know this, my son, although poet and seer, artist and musician make claim to this prophecy, they only serve to reveal the counterfeit of the real. God alone, who made the heavenly story given to the sages of the antediluvian world and taught to Noah, designed the great circle of stars that pass through the sun, telling the prophecy of the coming Son and the path of life in the age to come. All else is legend. All else is myth birthed from the corruptible seed of the dark one, that serpent of old, who continues to deceive as in the beginning. For only the Supreme Ruler of all things reveals the divine order and government of His dominion which increases and never ceases upon His shoulders, prophesying the story from beginning to the end. He has made Himself known to us and left us a witness in the heavenly lights that mark the signs and seasons and the appointed times. Even as man seeks His own way and attempts to make false claims about the heavenly images, the Children of Men who serve the Creator continue to give honor to Him who is the King of the Universe, bending knee and making confession to Him who guides man's destiny when he is awake or when deep sleep falls upon their heads.

> In a dream
> In a vision of the night

My instruction was sealed
I called for Wisdom and she spoke
to me of hidden treasures
I saw gates of bronze in pieces on the ground
And through double doors I stood before the
Potsherd
Who whispered in proverbial tone
"Can the clay be self-begotten or the
handiwork of the Potter form itself?" As I
drew closer
Upon a throne was the Ancient of Days
I stretched out my hands to receive a king's
armor
And the host of heaven shouted praises to
the One who created light and dispelled the
darkness
The One who is the Maker
Anointed my head and spoke to me of
subduing nations and
Overcoming the merchants of Egypt
Then I saw a great assembly gathered as an
army
I commanded them to free the exiles and
gather the plunder of
riches from the secret places
For by His hand my way was determined
To make the crooked places straight
In a dream
In a vision of the night.

The oracle of creation declares the truth about the Creator, my son. The Maker of the Universe created a world without form and void into a place of order, determining the years and days, appointed times and seasons. For as it is written:

> *He is supreme over all creation, because in connection with him were created all things — in heaven and on earth, visible and invisible, whether thrones, lordships, rulers or authorities — they have all been created through him and for him. He existed before all things, and he holds everything together.*

These foundational principles mark the beginning and reveal the One that unifies the cosmos, connecting the foundation of the worlds and permeating all realms with harmony and life. He is the essence that joins the spheres in heavenly places to all that is above and below, so that nothing exists without purpose, nothing exists without the unseen energy and light of His presence. His life energy emanates in all things. He is not of creation. All of creation is of Him.

Listen to me, my son, with humble hearts and in all sincerity we must come before the King of the Universe, expressing our adoration and worship. Let us stand like *oaks of righteousness, a planting of the Lord for the display of His splendor.* Like the Parable of the Trees, spoken by judges and temple priests, if we act in truth and sincerity about the king who reigns over us, all of nature will rejoice. *The trees of the field will clap their hands.* This is my deepest desire for you— to find your place in the heart of the King and the cosmos that He loves.

On Histories

Turn it and turn it again
for everything is in it
Pour over it and wax
grey and old over it

There are wells of knowledge, my son, concerning the depth of wonder about the histories of the Children of Men. I will share these truths with you that were spoken of when the Ancient of Days revealed them to man and to those who survived the waters that stretched out over the earth. In those days, when language was unified and the truth of creation told, the Maker of the Universe revealed His beauty in the patterns and sequences that generated mixtures, and mixtures then generated visible substances over time. These mysteries shared in stories and poems throughout the ages spoke of energy that sustained vegetation on the earth and unfolded like the petals of a flower that absorbed the rays of the sun.

This oracle speaks of a time when the ruler of darkness drove the people of the earth into deception. Only a remnant remained of those who held to the truth about the sovereignty of the King of the Universe. These were the days when battles had been fought in the heavens. In that season, the Maker shook the great circle above the skies and rent the veil that separated the waters above and the land below. The few that treasured the stories handed down to the sons of man set sail on the wind of God's Spirit to new lands. These were lands filled with promises of son-ship and rule with the King of the Universe. Those who mocked the Almighty and followed the heresies of principalities and powers were swept away in the fathoms below, but those who overcame the father of lies made an oath of consecration to Him who ruled the skies, declaring Him Lord of the whole world. The devoted ones of the King sang songs of love filling the heavens like a thousand years of prayer. He in turn descended upon them, speaking words of love in chorus to those with humble hearts who made allegiance to the King. Throughout the generations of times past to the present, from the time of the deluge until the time when language was scattered across the earth, the song of the I Am had been sung in remembrance of the days when the waters covered the earth.

> Come away with me
> The winter's gone and a time has come for singing
> Open up your eyes
> The rain has gone and a time has come for dreaming

Before the sands of time
I looked into your eyes
You may not understand
But I Am the reason that I love you
Listen to me
From East to West I can't see the past
anymore
Sail away with me
On summer winds we can find a better shore
Before the sands of time
I looked into your eyes
You may not understand
But I Am the reason that I love you
Nothing you do or say
Can make me change the way I feel about
you
You're always on my mind
And I'd like to say when I made the day
I thought of you
Before the sands of time
I looked into your eyes
You may not understand
But I Am the reason that I love you
I Am the reason that I love you.

At the time when the histories had been torn
asunder like two worlds divided, the remaining
peoples of the former habitation settled in new
realms, planting vineyards, establishing their fields
and praising the One who delivered them out of the

waters of the deluge, far from the place where the mighty men of old conjured spells and revealed the secret of making to the daughters of men. This new and fertile land, which the Creator birthed out of the flood and bestowed upon the faithful children of promise, would become the pinnacle to establish a new world. The patriarch, whose story is told in all lands throughout the ages, brought his sons and daughters through many days and nights on what seemed like endless seas. This righteous man, who survived the season of giants and the men of renown, had been given into his hands the secrets of the cosmos. These were the secrets that revealed the prophecies concerning the knowledge of the heavens and stars, the Wisdom of celestial patterns and the revelation of the end of days. And with one voice and in one accord, those who survived the waters that destroyed all living things, made an oath to raise the age-old foundations of their elders— an oath that beseeched them to carry the Wisdom of one truth and one language of the poetry of heaven across the vast divide of a time long forgotten and from a world swallowed in the abyss. This truth, given to the prophets of God to display His glory, would become their sacred word, not written on tablets of clay but on the hearts of men and arrayed in the cosmic fabric of time and the unlimited expanse.

These sages of antiquity knew the hidden knowledge of God's intention found in riddles and enigmas of His heavenly signs and upon the names of the antediluvian fathers. The signs were expressions found in the stars whose mark is on the righteous who dwell upon the earth. The mystery of these riddles and enigmas have been understood since the beginning of time, from the first man to the last patriarch, from star bound to star in the great circle of the heavens. The prophecy of His purpose was revealed to declare the great secrets that foretell the ways of the Father of lights. Signs and symbols are revealed in all of nature, whether seasons or epochs, or days when light increases upon the earth and then recedes again. The Ancient of Days bears witness to all He has created, revealing His goodness and mercy to the Children of Men. Though tribes and peoples, kings and nations adorn their temple halls with myth and legend, scribing in boastful voice some fable of their gods, the truth is displayed in the emblems of heaven and the signs that point the way to the Maker, for all these tales are but a shadow of the one, true light. He who is the source of all life is the standard by which all other forms are derived, for The King of Glory is the formidable answer to all inquiries about the nature of the universe. Though priests and princes try to sway you with their deceitful words, they are but fragments of truth weaved from the true cosmic tale of the genesis. Just as the sun returns again upon its course, so all of nature can be traced to its original source found only in the One. He is our breath, our life and our substance, though invisible in nature. He is ever present in the majesty He has displayed and made visible to our eyes by all He has established. We know this, my son, if with a humble heart we acknowledge that we are the many who are from the One. As mighty kings of old would claim on bended knee, *when I consider Your heavens, the work of Your fingers, the moon and the stars, which You ordained, what is man that You are mindful of him.* Those heroes, who captured in word and song the annals of the worlds and the principles of nature, sought only to know the ways of Him who holds the keys of heaven, to grasp a glimpse of the vast array of His Wisdom and to ascend to the heights of His presence where His glory is unveiled, for they knew that by understanding what power holds the worlds together is the first postulate in the study of cosmos.

As you knock on Wisdom's door my son and enter with a desire for understanding, she will reveal to you wonders found in the invisible realm of the pavilion of heaven. There, the substance that is not expressed by our senses is made evident, for there is harmony above and below reflected in shadows and types of all that is created, whether corporeal or incorporeal. Though my teaching may seem a paradox to your reasoning, it must be stated here that man cannot live by reason alone, for the King of the Universe is spirit, invisible, and He is one with all His attributes of beauty and order and gave design to the worlds in all realms. Such harmony rests in our souls from the breath He breathed into all mankind, for He made us in His image and patterned us to be like Him. Although He is all knowing, He has given us access so we can find our oneness in Him. The harmony of the universe, the patterns in nature sing through our very being and reflect the One who sings over us the truth of His power and glory. It is by faith resounding in our spirit that we become like a three-stranded cord bearing the evidence of His nature and things unseen.

Those who have gone before us were humbled by such knowledge my son, whether conqueror in battle or victor of legend and myth, and from their mouths came their rhetorical confession about their Maker and the grandeur of His being: *They saw the abyss and things secret, they opened the place hidden and carried back word of the time before the flood. Who can scale the heaven? As for men, their days are numbered; their achievements are a puff of wind.* From the conviction of their hearts they carved in stone their tales of old and sang them in lands where their liturgy was carried on the wind over mountains and over the ages. Those mystics of the antiquarian age wrote their meditations, recited them before common man and king as they sojourned to the thin places where portals open beyond the realms of this world. They sought to know the depth of secrets and hidden things concerning the primal nature of the universe and cosmic elements. As on a quest in search for treasure, they journeyed to far away lands, to Egypt and beyond, to understand the nature of God, His power and their destiny as cosmic beings. These learned minds filled themselves with knowledge from the storehouses of heaven, writing many a magnificent hymn about those who spoke of Him as Father of all.

Throughout the course of time, praises about the Maker of the Universe are found in picture or symbol on the walls and rooms of the middle earth or displayed on tombs. They are true adorations preserved by warriors, prophesied by seers, and heard in the cries of those who would not bow to envious lords as they fell to their death into the flames. For truly the wise know they are but vessels that carry His light. In all lands throughout the ages, man has given account of the manifest glory of Him who spoke all things into existence by the vibration of His word. More has been proclaimed of His splendor than all the chambers and chests of Alexandria could ever hope to hold.

> From the descending arm of heaven
> The Logos comes into the world
> To touch the minds of mortal man
> Who scribe illuminated words
> Like watchmen on the wall they guard
> The archives in this fertile storehouse

Sealed by oath and secret speech
To those who seek and knock and find
Hiding words of God's pure Wisdom
In jars of clay and in their hearts.

The adoration of God who is the Shepherd of
Men was unwavering by those who strived to seek
truth until the day when language was divided like
the waters that separated time and man in the
deluge. And in the season of the new dawn, when
the waters receded, the limitless presence of the
Maker poured out His love to reconcile man to
Himself and break down the dividing wall of
separation.

But prideful hearts were hardened against the
King of the Universe as men established their own
kingdoms and rule over the earth. It was a time
when man created images of gods to establish
power, when they made sacrifices to forms carved
in bronze and gold and worshiped trees and rivers
proclaimed as sacred in tales of old. Those who
established priestly disciplines and sacred offices
sought powers from the governors in heavenly
places, invoking the principalities of might and
dominion. They hoped to conjure with magic and
sorcery the keys to the mysteries and secrets of the
One whose Wisdom is far above all worlds and
whose power is above creation, *for all things were put
under His feet.* These dreams and vain imaginations
became the raiment of kings who desired the

people of their rule to bend a knee to their greatness, which they claimed was mirrored in the stars. Yet all who were wise knew that the visible form was a mere reflection of the invisible reality of God's majesty and wonder. *For the likeness, whether in flesh or in spiritual existence, is not the reality, but the shadow; and the shadow may well bow down before the substance.* Those ignorant of such spiritual matters, who had sleeping hearts, did not comprehend the song of the stars that spoke of the prophecy of the Sovereign Ruler of the Universe. He Himself ordained the emblems of the heavens to bear witness of His glory and to declare the path of His righteousness. But foolish man worshiped the emblems themselves and instructed their disciples to set a course on destiny's wings, which were bound to patterns and celestial signs of their making.

Many are the dedications and tributes that bear witness to God's glory revealed in the heavens and upon the earth, in signs made of stone and structures of wood, whether temple or circle. From the wisest of men to those considered by learned men as barbarian, each one established memorial to the majesty of the King of the Universe and His creation. Long before these stories were written on papyri or clay, they were told in oral traditions and spoken of as secret knowledge. The sacred stories of old were passed down as Wisdom of the astronomer priests, those who taught their disciples using symbol in nature to reveal the knowledge of the heavens about motion, patterns, divine proportions and the relationship of the cosmic lights and spheres with music, seasons and appointed times. These earth signs that man had made were created to establish a visible understanding of the invisible world. Whether stone circle or ceremonial structure hidden in groves, their common purpose was to mirror the sky above allowing man to ponder the world, to measure his days, and to gain understanding of the nature of the universe. Yet, a day had come when man sought his own intention, building towers to gain access to the heavens. Sacred structures became the places of ceremony on a midsummer's night to those who sought the mystic center of the universe with a passion to invoke the powers above and set up dominion over kingdoms and rulers on the earth below. The priests who instructed kings about the opposing, cosmic forces shared their knowledge concerning the duality of symbol, prophesied about omens found in the nature of good and evil, dark and light. Such dark omens weighed heavy on those who lacked understanding, creating fear in the hearts of those who could no longer remember the time when the Ancient of Days cast the dark one and his army from heaven. As the offspring of chaos covered the earth and gross darkness covered the people, those who pledged devotion to religious rite and magic art established generation upon generation of tales by which the gods of the seas and skies would fight the battle between the opposing powers of good and evil. Those who wore the sacred robes would build fires with eternal flames and sacred wells and altars in hopes of conjuring spells and spirits to protect them, believing that when the moon waxed or waned they could arouse nature from her sleep. Their tales were weaved with superstitions that shrouded them like a night mist, for those who believed them true felt haunted by the need to appease the spirits of the otherworld with gold tossed in rivers and wells or by catching sacred fish or birds that might bring them Wisdom and good fortune. The astronomer priests fed the common man on the bread of enchantments, breeding lies through ritual and divination, building fires and altars of stone at twilight in search of the mystic center of the world.

These grounds known to many as thin spaces, were places where kingly priests endeavored to replicate the ancient Wisdom of the universe, places where the collective power of stones and mounds, sacred groves and temples mirrored the stars in a magnificent balance between heaven and earth. Wherever these places were found across the earth, there were battles and sacrifice, giants and ritual. Designed originally to reflect in worship the beauty of the created universe of the Maker, they had now become the places of captivity and bondage of depraved minds. Though many were warned by priests and prophets of the coming destruction, few listened as in the days of Noah, for they had become impious in all their ways, believing the blind god, and ignoring the prophetic utterance:

Those who forsake the Lord shall be consumed. For they shall be ashamed of the sacred trees which you have desired; and you shall be embarrassed because of the gardens which you have chosen. For you shall be as a sacred tree whose leaf fades, and as a garden that has no water.

For God Himself warned them of the crafty one and what would become of his multitude for leading astray the Children of Men. For many fell prey to deception and blasphemed the Divine. The King of the Universe challenged them about their enchantments and their sorcery. He had become weary of those who worshipped idols and the forces presiding over darkness, those astrologers and stargazers who sought help and power from God's created luminaries above and from the signs upon the earth that man had made to mirror their image.

These are the histories and chronicles of the Children of Men. Like in ages past, history spirals through time into the current age and truth slips away like a mist on a moonlit lake. So guard your heart, my son. Many will come with deceptive and hollow philosophies claiming to understand the powers and forces of the cosmos, but only the Maker of the Universe is worthy to have the majesty and the glory forever. Seek out for yourself the truth that I have shared with you. Only the truth will set you free.

So I seal the words of this oracle with a prophetic declaration over your life. May the kingdom of heaven fall upon you, and the revelation of God's purpose open to you. May the illumination of His truth fill you like an earthen vessel, overflowing with goodness. May you be blessed with every heavenly blessing of wisdom, power and might as you come to know the ways of the King of the Universe and His destiny for your life. May doors open to you that no man can shut as you become enlightened by the mysteries and secrets whispered in the shade of the Elder Tree.

Bibliography

Celtic Studies

Ashe, Geoffrey. *Mythology of the British Isles*. London: Methuen, 2002. Print.

Ashe, Geoffrey. *King Arthur's Avalon: The Story of Glastonbury*. Gloucestershire: Sutton, 2007. Print.

Brennan, Martin. *The Stones of Time: Calendars, Sundials, and Stone Chambers of Ancient Ireland*. Rochester, VT: Inner Traditions, 1994. Print.

Bridgman, Timothy P. *Hyperboreans: Myth and History in Celtic-Hellenic Contacts*. London: Routledge, 2011. Print.

Ellis, Peter Berresford. *A Brief History of the Druids*. New York: Carroll & Graf, 2002. Print.

Hawkins, Gerald S., and John B. White. *Stonehenge Decoded: an Astronomer Examines One of the Great Puzzles of the Ancient World*. [S.l.]: Barnes & Noble, 1965. Print.

Heath, Robin, and John F. Michell. *The Lost Science of Measuring the Earth: Discovering the Sacred Geometry of the Ancients*. Kempton, IL: Adventures Unlimited, 2006. Print.

Markale, Jean. *The Celts: Uncovering the Mythic and Historic Origins of Western Culture*. Rochester, VT: Inner Traditions, 1993. Print.

Miranda Green. *The Celtic World*. Abe Books, 2012. Print

Melrose, Robin. *The Druids and King Arthur: A New View of Early Britain*. Jefferson, NC: McFarland, 2011. Print.

Michell, John. *Secrets of the Stones: New Revelations of Astro-archaeology and the Mystical Sciences of Antiquity*. Rochester, VT: Inner Traditions International, 1989. Print.

Piggott, Stuart. *Ancient Britons and the Antiquarian Imagination: Ideas from the Renaissance to the Regency*. [London]: Thames and Hudson, 1989. Print.

Proinsias, MacCana. *Celtic Mythology*. 2012 Print. Proinsias, MacCana.

Rees, Alwyn and Brinley. *Celtic Heritage*. Thames and Hudson, 1961. Print

Squire, Charles. *Celtic Myth and Legends*. Bristol: Parragon Books, 1998.Print

Orphic Studies

Athanassakis, Apostolos N. *The Homeric Hymns*. Baltimore: Johns Hopkins UP, 2004. Print.

Cahill, Thomas. *Sailing the Wine-Dark Sea: Why the Greeks Matter. Barnes & Noble*. N.p., n.d. Web. 18 July 2013.

Fideler, David R. *Jesus Christ, Sun of God: Ancient Cosmology and Early Christian Symbolism*. Wheaton, IL: Quest, 1993. Print

Guthrie, W. K. C. *Orpheus and Greek Religion: A Study of the Orphic Movement*. Princeton, NJ: Princeton UP, 1993. Print.

Guthrie, Kenneth Sylvan, and David R. Fideler. *The Pythagorean Sourcebook and Library: An Anthology of Ancient Writings Which Relate to Pythagoras and Pythagorean Philosophy*. Grand Rapids: Phanes, 1987. Print.

Herodotus, Robert B. Strassler, and Andrea L. Purvis. *The Landmark Herodotus: The Histories*. New York: Anchor, 2009. Print.

Josephus, Flavius, and William Whiston. *The Works of Josephus: Complete and Unabridged*. Peabody, MA: Hendrickson, 1987. Print.

Kingsley, Peter. *Ancient Philosophy, Mystery, and Magic: Empedocles and Pythagorean Tradition*. Oxford: Clarendon, 1995. Print.

Philo, and Charles Duke Yonge. *The Works of Philo: Complete and Unabridged*. Peabody, MA: Hendrickson Pub. 1993. Print.

Taylor, Thomas. *Plato: The Timaeus, and the Critias: Or Atlanticus*. United States: Kessinger, 2006. Print.

Strachan, Gordon. *Jesus the Master Builder: Druid Mysteries and the Dawn of Christianity*. Edinburgh: Floris, 2001. Print.

Strohmeier, John, and Peter Westbrook. *Divine Harmony: The Life and Teachings of Pythagoras*. Berkeley, CA: Berkeley Hills, 1999. Print.

Taylor, Thomas. *The Hymns of Orpheus: With the Life and Theology of Orpheus*. Forgotten Books. 2012. Print.

Jewish Studies

Bullinger, E.W. *The Witness of The Stars.* N.p., n.d. Web. 16 July 2013. "Lectures on the Sacred Poetry of the Hebrews." By Lowth, Robert.

Cahill, Thomas. *The Gifts of the Jews: How a Tribe of Desert Nomads Changed the Way Everyone Thinks and Feels: Amazon.com: Books.* N.p., n.d. Web. 18 July 2013.

Charles R.H. *The Book Of The Secrets Of Enoch. W. R. Morfill: Books.* N.p., n.d. Web. 16 July 2013.

Charles, R.H.: *The Book of Jubilees or the Little Genesis): R. H. Charles: Books.* N.p., n.d. Web. 16 July 2013.

Cohen, Abraham: *Everyman's Talmud: The Major Teachings of the Rabbinic Sages Abraham Cohen: Books.* N.p., n.d. Web. 16 July 2013.

Chumney, EdwardThe *The Seven Festivals of the Messiah: Amazon.com: Books.* N.p., n.d. Web. 17 July 2013.

Conner, Kevin J. *The Feasts of Israel:Amazon.com: Books.* N.p., n.d. Web. 17 July 2013.

Munder, Walter E. *Astronomy of the Bible: Amazon.com: Books.* N.p., n.d. Web. 17 July 2013.

Rolleston, Frances. *Mazzaroth, Or, The Constellations.* York Beach, ME: Weiser, 2001. Print.

Salaman., Nina *Selected poems of Jehudah Halevi.* The Jewish Publication Society. 1928. Print.

Scholem, Gershom "*Zohar: The Book of Splendor: Basic Readings from the Kabbalah.*". N.p., n.d. Web.

17 July 2013.

Strachan, Gordon. *The Bible's Hidden Cosmology: Amazon.co.uk: Gordon Strachan Books*. N.p., n.d. Web. 16 July 2013.

Milton, Terry. *The Sibylline Oracles. Elfinspell: Online Intro, Sibylline Oracles, Milton S. Terry English Translation, Online Text, Early Christianity, Apocalyptic Literature, Ancient Greek and Rome Religion,*. N.p., n.d. Web. 18 July 2013.

Yosef Wineberg, Levi Wineberg, Uri Kaploun, Sholom Wineberg: *Lessons in Tanya (5 Vols): 9780826605405: Amazon.com: Books*. N.p., n.d. Web. 16 July 2013.

Yourgrau, Palle. *A World without Time: The Forgotten Legacy of Gödel and Einstein*. New York: Basic, 2005. Print.

Endnotes

On Wisdom
Art illustration verses: Proverbs 1:5-6
Pages 1-14 Like many early writers, the
thoughts contained in these pages reflect a
syncretism of ideas. The philosophical
history of the time was established around
oral traditions and Wisdom letters mainly to
students or disciples of the study of
cosmology. Within the scope of feminine
connotation and imagery is the theme of
Wisdom in sacred text. Though many
traditions speak of this imagery, both
Hebrew and Orphic emphasize the concept.
Whereas Wisdom is personified in Greek,
Hermetic and Celtic culture as a female
figure, Hebrew tradition emphasizes a
feminine nature linguistically expressing a
structural style. Wisdom in this context is an
attribute of God's nature that is separate
from the worldly understanding as
mentioned in the Teachings of Silvanus,
"Where is a man who is wise or powerful in
intelligence, or a man whose devices are
many because he knows Wisdom? Let him
speak Wisdom; let him utter great boasting!
For every man has become a fool and has
spoken out of his own knowledge" (The Nag
Hammadi Library in English 392). Elder Tree

explores the nature of Wisdom and the many aspects that Wisdom offers us if we follow her path. Divine Wisdom is discovered in the higher realms; the upper spheres of illumination where one begins to understand the ways of God. In contrast, Wisdom that is personified takes on a divine nature in its own right. As a feminine force, Wisdom becomes that which creates and establishes things within creation and is named Sophia. See section of the Nag Hammadi Scripture on the Origins of the World. Wisdom also plays the role of assisting those who seek her council to ascend to higher realms of understanding in order to gain illumination about the mysteries and secrets of the universe. This is a reoccurring theme in the Tanya of ascending to realms above the faculty of reason to attain Wisdom that comes from God alone.

The Oracle is written as a collection of religious texts that have an emphasis on prophetic understanding of the cosmos. Similar in format to the Nag Hammadi Scriptures, which is rooted in both primitive interpretations of cosmology and antediluvian philosophy, the contents of this book are more constructive than critical. This creative approach of speaking about the secret Wisdom of Elder Tree philosophy is at the heart of these traditions. "They offered reasons for their opinions, they gave arguments for their views. They did not utter *ex cathedra* pronouncements. Or rather and more modestly: most of the thinkers were, for most of the time, concerned not to advance opinions but to advance reasoned opinions" (Early Greek Philosophy 25). Spoken by a prophetess known as "The Oracle", the language used to express these opinions in Book I are written in prose with poetic interludes. She speaks revealing the Wisdom of the ancients and the mysteries that surround the King and Maker of the Universe. Her tale spans the various cultures familiar with heavenly inspiration of the Elder Tree, a mystical concept and reference to the disciples and initiates who knew the secrets of the cosmos and the nature of God. For further reading see Jesus Christ Sun of God by David Fideler, The Sibylline Oracles and The Greek Philosophers by W.K. Guthrie to cite examples of this widespread understanding.

The italicized references are in chronological order as follows:

Page 7: Colossians 1:17. Psalm 1:3. Proverbs 3:19

Page 8: The Sibylline Oracles by Milton

Page 11: Romans 11:35

Page 14: Ephesians 2:15
Page 15: Ephesians 3:17-19. Psalm 45:1

On Light

Art illustration verse: Job 26:10
Pages 15-23
These pages of the Oracle are constructed to
define and express the essence of created
light and the distinctions of the light of
God's nature. Throughout this section are
references to the types of light and their
function as demonstrated in creation. Light
has both a physical and esoteric connotation
for life and living.

Concerning the concept of "one language"
mentioned throughout this book, especially
in the epistle on Wisdom, we find that the
ancients believed in an order that was
established by the Maker of the Universe by
His light and word. This language specifically
speaks of how the things in the universe
were formed and placed in an orderly fashion
by the one and only entity, which is God.
References are made to sequential patterns
and alchemy revealing the intent of God's
order and plan that entails the nature of life
in creation. As stated by in the Tanya,
"Understand clearly that every creature and
being, is in reality considered to be absolute
naught and nothingness in relation to the

activating force which creates it and the breath of His mouth continuously calling into existence and bringing it from absolute non-being into being" (Tanya Book3 851). The language of God, which is the word of God, logos, arithmos, was revealed to humanity in many ways through shadows and types. One form in particular demonstrating the symbolism of language was through the constellations known as the Mazzaroth. This language was known and expressed in many cultures by means of pictorial stories that bear witness to the original names and the prophetic meaning behind the stars. Though there are various interpretations and expressions of the meaning conveyed in cultures about the luminaries, the general commonality is one of prophecy. According to Francis Rolleston, "Abundant evidence exists that the explanation of these emblems by prophecy is no new system, not theory spun from raw materials, but a thread of gold, unraveled from an ancient and superb tissue, originating with the early patriarchs, in which as in the embroidery of old, were interwoven the records they desires to transmit" (Mazzaroth 15). These orbs that declared their poetry of heaven was a part of an antediluvian language of sign and symbol that would guide those on their journeys and establish a belief system in the chronology of the cosmic order. Though these signs were known by the nations and throughout the ages, the original form changed as dark wisdom and deception veiled the original purpose. This was expressed explicitly in the Nag Hammadi texts that gave various names to the "dark one" or "blind god", the equivalent to Satan, Lucifer or the serpent in scripture, the ancient traditions all expressed some form of evil and corruptible force to try and harness the power of the governors of the sky. These terms are mentioned in the text titled Origins of the world in which imagery is conveyed about the verbal expression to create and the corruption of the original order by the dark Wisdom of the ages. (The Nag Hammadi Library in English 172-175). For further reading see E.W. Bullinger's book, Witness of the Stars.

The italicized references are in chronological order as follows:
Page 18: Psalm 36:9. John 14:6.
Page 20: Psalm 119:2

On Creation
Art illustration verses: Job 26:13-14
Pages 25-35

The next several pages are dedicated to concepts related to the nature of God and adoration of the King of the Universe. The pages are flavored with poems and songs showing devotion to the Creator and His creation. The ancient traditions share a common theme of praising the one who made the cosmos, from Hermes and Orpheus to Hebrew poetry that reflects the imagery of harmony and design. Harmony and unity are major themes in Pythagorean understanding. For further study see the Hymns of Hermes, the Hymns of Orpheus and The Pythagorean Sourcebook by Kenneth Guthrie.

Throughout the traditions, knowledge of the world and the cosmological framework were seen through an expanded view of nature. " When the Presocratics inquired into 'nature', they were not only inquiring into the natural world—they were inquiring into 'the natures of things'" (Early Greek Philosophy 21). Science was believed to have an orderly arrangement with spiritual implications. The thought of the time was to give definition to that order through various perspectives on the physical elements and the genesis of life. As W.K Guthrie wrote, "We shall be speaking of a time when science and philosophy were both in their infancy and no line was drawn between them" (The Greek

Philosophers 16).

Also in this section is the imagery and expressions of nature that can be found in the Celtic tradition. Though each culture has its own concept of power and forces, the Celtic tradition stresses places in nature where heaven meets earth in "thin places" or "mystic centers", near groves or oak tress. " The Celt as the seeker after God, linked himself to strong ties to the unseen, and eager to conquer the unknown by religious rite or magic art" (The Druids 113). Threads of similar practice are weaved through the Hermetic and Orphic as well, though not without those who gave fair warning and apocalyptic prophecy about those who practiced means of attaining power for selfish ambition or idolatry, which can be seen in Asclepius and other texts of the Hermetic tradition. (See The Nag Hammadi Library in English 334-335). Here one sees the chasm between good and evil, dark and light and the advice of the Oracle to use clear judgment and seek Wisdom so as not to be deceived. These aspects of nature are reflected in the various names of God and His counterfeit and the deceiver of truth. Throughout these traditions, many names are given to represent the one eternal God and many names were used to express the nature of the evil one who sought to destroy all that is beautiful and orderly in creation. This epistle stresses that desire of God for His creation pattern after his design to establish harmony of his soul with the Creator. Music is one aspect of imagery used to describe oneness. Other aspects of nature are also used metaphorically such as trees. Trees were consistently used in ancient traditions to express wisdom, righteousness and knowledge from the invisible realm of heaven. There is a lot of imagery of trees in this section to build on the Elder Tree Wisdom and folklore of the time.

The italicized references are in chronological order as follows:

Page 24: Matthew 6:13. *Selected poems of Jehudah Halevi.* By Nina Salaman

Page 26: Genesis 3:15

Page 27: Colossians 1:16-17

Page 28: Isaiah 61:3. Isaiah 55:12

On Histories

Art illustration verses: The Tanya Book III

Pages 37-52

There is an amazing common origin that all cultures in some respect seem to share—the story of the flood. Gilgamesh speaks of such a time, and throughout all of antiquity there is a familiar concept of a time when the world was engulfed by water. The origin of these roots is found in Hebrew literature, but all these traditions share a belief in a primordial upheaval of nature. The antiquarian tale seems to surpass myth. " The surest and best characteristic of a well-founded and extensive induction is, when verifications of it spring up, as it were, spontaneously into notice, from quarters where they be least expected, or from among instances of that very kind which were at first considered hostile to them. Evidence of this kind is irresistible, and compels assent with a weight that scarcely any other possesses" (Mazzaroth 12).

This same chronology of an original language seemed to be mysteriously coded in various aspects of nature prior to the deluge. This language established a prophetic message in nature for the ages to come and establishing forethought that demonstrates sovereignty about the origins of the cosmos. The implication throughout the epistle on Histories is that only fragments of this mysterious language and understanding remained after the evil one weaved deception into the thoughts of man. As life expanded on the planet, man was disillusioned about the truth of the genesis and began to orchestrate his own understanding of the origin of the universe.

At this point in time, superstition, magic and divination infiltrated the thinking of man who sought his own way and sought for power in the cosmic forces. Here the oracle warns that in every season and every age, man has sought to find his way apart from God who is the only true source of life and understanding. Time spirals back around from one age to another with this same concern expressing as Solomon that there is nothing new under that sun.

The italicized references are in chronological order as follows:

Page 33: Psalm 8:3-4

Page 34: Gilgamesh 57 and 109

Page 36: Ephesians 1:21-23.

The Mazzaroth by Francis Rolleston 53.

Page 38: Isaiah 1:28-30